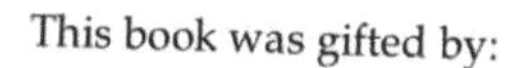

The mission of the Will James Society is:

"To promote the Legacy, Literature and Art of the Great Cowboy author, Will James, through the gifting of his inspirational books to schools, public libraries, our military units and hospitals throughout the world, and other interested and worthy institutions."

Visit our website at:
www.WillJames.org
or write to:
Will James Society
PO Box 1572
Elko, NV 89803

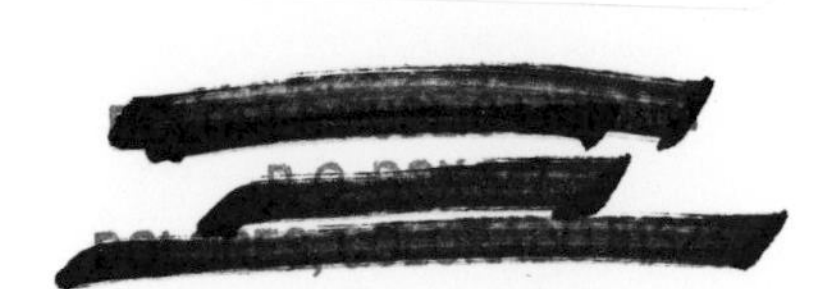

YOUNG COWBOY

Then trouble broke loose. –Art courtesy of Tom Decker

YOUNG COWBOY

By Will James

Arranged from *Big-Enough* and *Sun Up*
Illustrated by the Author

MOUNTAIN PRESS PUBLISHING COMPANY • MISSOULA, MONTANA • 2000

Second Printing, March 2008

Color plate on page 27. *The Hiss of the Rope* (alternate title: *Smoky and the Snubbing Post*). Oil on canvas, 1929. Gift of Virginia Snook to the Yellowstone Art Museum. Reprinted with permission of the Will James Art Company.

Color plate on page 47. *Cheer of Home Fires Not for the Wanted.* Oil on canvas, 1929. Gift of Virginia Snook to the Yellowstone Art Museum. Reprinted with permission of the Will James Art Company.

Cover design by Kim Ericsson.

Tumbleweed Series is a registered trademark of Mountain Press Publishing Company.

Library of Congress Cataloging-in-Publication Data

James, Will, 1892–1942.
Young cowboy / by Will James ; arranged from "Big-Enough" and "Sun up" ; illustrated by the author.
p. cm. – (Tumbleweed series)
Summary: Having gotten his first horse, Big-Enough, for his fourth birthday, Billy spends the next several years working hard to become a good, all-around cowboy on his father's ranch.
ISBN 0-87842-419-9
[1. Cowboys—Fiction. 2. Ranch life—Fiction. 3. Horses—Fiction.] I. Title
PZ7.J1545 Yo 2000
[Fic]—dc21 00-010304

PRINTED IN HONG KONG BY MANTEC PRODUCTION COMPANY

MOUNTAIN PRESS PUBLISHING COMPANY
P. O. Box 2399 • Missoula, Montana 59806 • (406) 728-1900

Publisher's Note

Will James's books are an American treasure. His writing and drawings captivated generations of readers with the lifestyle and spirit of the American cowboy and the West. Following James's death in 1942, the reputation of this remarkable writer and artist languished, and nearly all of his twenty-four books went out of print. But in recent years, publication of several biographies and film documentaries on James, public exhibitions of his art, and the formation of the Will James Society have renewed interest in his work.

Now, in conjunction with the Will James Art Company, Mountain Press is reprinting all Will James's books under the name the Tumbleweed Series, taking special care to keep each volume faithful to the original. Books in the Tumbleweed Series contain all the original artwork and text, feature an attractive new design, and are printed on acid-free paper.

Charles Scribner's Sons, James's first publisher, arranged and modified a few of James's earlier stories into *Young Cowboy* and published it in 1935. This children's book combines the first six chapters of *Big-Enough* and the short story "The Young Cowboy" from *Sun Up*.

The republication of Will James's books would not have been possible without the help and support of the many fans of Will James. Because all James's books and artwork remain under copyright protection, the Will James Art Company has been instrumental in providing the necessary permissions and furnishing artwork. Tom Decker furnished the original art for the cover and frontispiece of *Young Cowboy*, and the Yellowstone Art Museum in Billings, Montana, provided the original art for two of the color plates.

The Will James Society was formed in 1992 as a nonprofit organization dedicated to preserving the memory and works of Will James. The society is one of the primary catalysts behind a growing interest not only in Will James and his work, but also in the life and heritage of the working cowboy. For more information on the society, contact:

Will James Society
P.O. Box 1572
Elko, NV 89803

WillJamesSociety@yahoo.com
WillJames.org

Mountain Press is pleased to make Will James's books available again. Read and enjoy!

JOHN RIMEL

Illustrations

Then trouble broke loose. (frontispiece) ii
The little feller. 3
Billy and his Dad. 5
Jim found the colt quite a few miles from home. 6
Billy in the snow. 8
Jim taught him walking alongside. 9
Jim stirred up quite a surprise. 12
That saddle meant a heap more to Billy than any shiny automobile or airplane could mean to any kid. 16
With Christmas came a little pair of boots. 21
Tied up and thinking it over. 22
Letting him run around the snubbing post. 23
The quirt takes the buck out of him. 24
All they needed was riding among the herds. 25
Bucking even harder than before. 26
Watching the rider rope one wild range horse after another. (color) 27
They rode all day. 30
The chuck wagon. 32
There were lots of bulls fighting in that big herd. 37
She made a pass at his horse and then a loop settled on her horns. (color) 39
Her head was brought to snap alongside of her tail, she was raised four feet off the ground. 43
In winter. (color) 47
Pictures of everything to attract the cowboy's eye. 50
He thought sure the end had come. 55
Town was reached in less than three hours. 57
He wondered how Big-Enough had wintered and what he looked like. (color) 61
Big-Enough had come in from the pasture that evening. 63
The little horse was bucking pretty good. 70

Chapter One

"Sure is wet," said Jim, the cowboy. He slid his horse down a slippery hill and headed him towards a ranch house on the creek. "Think I'll drop in on Lem and dry up a bit."

As the cowboy rode up to the ranch house Lem opened the door.

"You're just in time, Jim. A little Roper has just come to our house and you can do the honors of giving him a first name. Never mind that mud on your heels, hang up your slicker and come on in."

The rain was still pouring down and it was late in the afternoon when a name was finally agreed on for the little fellow. Even Mrs. Roper after thinking up a lot of long and fancy names came to agree with Jim and Lem that William would do. The boy himself let out a good long squawk as much as to say he thought it would do, too.

The name being decided on, Jim went back to the shed, got on his horse and rode away.

The cowboy's horse was slipping along through a grove of trees when he heard leaves rustle to one side. There was a mare, shivering under the cold spring rain and trying to get her brand new little colt to follow her. The colt was shivering too, and dripping wet.

"By golly," said Jim, "this kind of weather is enough to stunt that little feller. Think I'll run him into camp and shove him under the shed where it is dry. Daggone if he don't look like he's just a few hours old, maybe born on the same minute that little Billy Roper was."

So Jim got the colt and mare past the corral gate and then under the big dry shed.

Many inches of snow covered the ground the next morning and a raw wind began to blow. Jim forked some good hay to the snorting mare and noticed that the colt was up and dry with eyes shining. "Sure am glad I run acrost you, little feller," he said. "This snow would of been kind of tough on you."

The little feller

Chapter Two

The colt grew and little Billy Roper grew. Billy took to riding as easy as a duck takes to water. His dad put a quilt in front of the saddle and took him for short rides when he was less than a year old, and many short and longer ones after that.

The colt was a fine looking yearling, small but a lot wiser than any twice his age.

"He'll sure make a fine horse for little Billy," Jim often thought. "When the colt is four years old Billy will be four too. The colt will be at a good age to break and Billy will be at a good age to start riding. I'll start breaking him right now, so he'll be good and gentle when the kid gets him."

Jim went into the stable and brought out an old saddle. With it in his right hand he started toward the colt.

The colt was already gentle, he'd got so he followed the cowboy all around and was often in the way. But when he saw that saddle coming he knew right away something was up that was strange. He wouldn't let the cowboy come near him. It wasn't until Jim had got a rope over the colt's neck and drawn it up that he could get near.

Jim laughed as he eased the saddle on the colt's back. The colt's little body was quivering and he was snorting like a good one.

"Regular little wild horse, ain't you?" Jim grinned.

The weight of the saddle on the colt was no more than a coat would be to a person. But he didn't know what to make of it and when he looked back to see that strange thing on him with stirrups flapping on both sides he was rearing to get away from under all of that.

The cowboy slackened up on the rope and let him go. When the colt got to the end of the rope he let out the finest little beller a colt of his size could make. Then he went to

Billy and his Dad

Jim found the colt quite a few miles from home.

wiping the earth with himself and that saddle. He'd go up in the air, let out a beller and come down on his side, sometimes on his neck and shoulders. He'd bounce up again and go to it some more, till finally he stood up quivering and out of breath. Then he began reaching on each side of him and biting the stirrup leathers.

"That wouldn't be so good for a feller's leg if it was there," Jim said. "You'd get your nose slapped doing that."

After resting a spell and staring around wild-eyed the colt went to bucking once more. That was the only way he could think of getting rid of that hunk of leather on top of him. But that hunk of leather stuck and the bucking spells began to get shorter, further apart and less wicked. Finally he went to trotting around, slowed down to a jerky walk and then stood still.

Jim left the saddle on him for an hour that day. The colt bucked some more after he took it off, he wanted to make sure it was off.

Every day the colt got his lesson with the saddle and every day his bad acting got to be less and less. He got to behaving so well after a couple of weeks time that he could be caught and saddled without having to be roped. He finally got so he never looked back at the saddle and so he would even eat his hay and grass while it was on his back.

One fine spring day when the snow was most all gone and the grass was fast getting green, Jim rode back to camp to find the colt quite a few miles from home, heading toward a bunch of horses not far away.

Jim stopped his horse and watched him. "Well, little feller, I'll let you go now. You can go for all summer and keep your tummy full of good grass and water. I'll find you again when the snows begin to fall."

Billy in the snow

Chapter Three

Winter came. Anybody who rode past the Ropers' ranch house during any day that winter saw little Billy all bundled up and playing in the snow.

At Jim's camp the colt was packing a saddle around the corral. When the wind howled and the snow drifted the colt wasn't bothered much with his saddle education.

In the spring when the snow was melting away the colt was just as used to the saddle as he was to his tail. Now something new had been brought up which he had to get used to. It was a bridle. A light snaffle bit was slipped in his mouth and with that thing pulled at by the cowboy, one way and another he had to learn to turn, stop and go when he was wanted to. He fought the bit at first, wouldn't turn or do anything. The cowboy along side of him jabbed him with his knee a few times and finally got him to moving. Then Jim taught him the ways of the rein. He never got in the saddle once, for the colt was too small, so Jim taught him while on the ground walking alongside.

"You little runt," Jim said. "You'll turn out to be a good horse some day if you ever get big enough."

Jim taught him walking alongside.

Chapter Four

Summer passed well with the colt the same as it did with little Billy Roper. The next spring was the colt's fourth spring and Jim went on with his education. He seemed to know everything now but being sat on. Jim hated to get on him, he was so small. But one day he dragged out his saddle, and grinning kind of foolish like, he cinched it on the colt. He looked all around to see if anybody might be riding up and then, with spurs nearly dragging the ground he started the colt out.

There was a surprise due him. He was riding along and watching the country around him when the colt of a sudden tied himself up in a knot. That colt seemed to be everywhere and nowhere all at once and the first thing Jim knew he was on the ground hanging on to one rein.

Jim figured that bucking would have to be taken out of him or he'd never do for Billy. So he saddled and rode the colt for a little while every day. It took quite a few whippings to make the colt forget the ideas that were in his head, but after a time he showed no sign that there'd ever been a buck in him.

Jim thought the colt would do now. It was somewhere close to the time the colt was turning four years old when Jim slipped a hackamore on him and getting on his horse, started to lead him away. He rode on and headed straight for Lem Roper's ranch. Jim had figured and planned a long time for this day. Every night for a month he'd crossed out the date of a day gone so that the day he was watching for wouldn't slip by without his knowing. That day was little Billy Roper's birthday, his fourth one, and Jim wanted to surprise the kid with the colt that day.

Not even Lem knew of the plan that Jim had been shaping up. So when Jim rode around the corner of the stables he stirred up quite a surprise.

"Well Jim," Lem laughed, "Where are you going with that half-pint? Why don't you put it in your pocket?"

"I got to keep that pocket space for my tobacco," Jim grinned back. "But what do you think of him, Lem? Come look him over."

"Sure a cute little feller," said Lem.

"I sure thought so and he's gentle too. I brought him over for little Billy for his birthday present."

Jim stirred up quite a surprise.

"For Billy?" Lem stuttered for a spell but finally managed to say, "By golly, that's sure fine, Jim, and Billy will sure be tickled." Lem glanced towards the house. "But the poor little devil is a bit under the weather now, tho, got the mumps or something."

Lem looked up to see a disappointed look on Jim's face. Jim had been anxious to see how Billy would act when he saw the colt.

"Well let's go up to the house anyway," said Lem. "Billy can look at his horse through the window."

Billy no more than got a glance at the colt and was told he was his for keeps than the house got to be a heap too small for him. He didn't want a window between him and his horse. He finally had to be bundled up and let out and he sure was a pleased kid when he was hoisted up on the round back of the little bay.

"By golly, that's one of the smallest horses I ever seen," said Lem. "But he's dandy for Billy and he'll do him fine till he gets tall enough for a bigger horse."

"He'll be big enough for Billy any time," said Jim. "He'll grow quite a bit yet and be plenty big enough." Jim was quiet for a minute and then went on.

"Say Lem, I just happened to stumble onto a good name for that little horse. I've thought of Cricket, Grasshopper, and such names as that, but them names

don't mean anything. What do you say we call him Big-Enough? That sure fits him all around and some day I know he'll be living up to his name. Big-Enough for most anything."

So Big-Enough was the name that was fastened on the little bay colt. Billy didn't mind the name, only it was hard to say, and the closest he could get to it was "Big-nuff."

Chapter Five

The next day there seemed to be no mumps or anything the matter with Billy. After a lot of coaxing he got his mother to let him go to the corral. He found his dad there by the stable door trying to cut down an old saddle to fit Billy. There was a lot of cutting to be done and small stirrups to be made. Late that afternoon Billy had a saddle that would do him. Lem wished that he'd got the kid a little saddle the last time he was in town, but he'd never thought much of saddles for Billy. Anyway, being now he had a horse his size, he'd get him one to match him when he made his next trip in.

Lem showed Billy just how to get Big-Enough next to a pole or rock and hold him there when he climbed on. Billy didn't have to be shown how to climb on more than once. He didn't let go of his bridle reins either, for he seemed already to know that letting go of them was a good way to be left afoot if the horse started too soon.

That saddle meant a heap more to Billy than any shiny automobile or airplane could mean to any kid.

It was a great day for Billy when one day, after his dad had come back from town, he went down to the corral to saddle Big-Enough and found him in the stable already saddled. He was saddled not with the old one Billy had been using but with a brand new little bitty one just his size. The sight of that new little saddle with the fancy flower-stamped leather and all made him stop, stary-eyed. Finally he began to sort of tiptoe up to it, as if it might get away from him if he rushed up.

Lem and his wife were hid in a stall not far away, watching Billy. They watched him come up to the saddle. He stood back and looked at it, reached and touched it, rubbed his hands over the new leather and felt the flower stamping, the cantle, the horn and all that was part of it. Every once in a while he'd stand back and just look it over, and then he'd come to it again and finger it some more.

That saddle meant a heap more to Billy than any shiny automobile or airplane could mean to any kid. It was bred in him to love saddle leather.

Billy finally untied Big-Enough, and all the way out of the stable into the corral he looked back to see how the stirrups hung and how the saddle set. And he didn't get on in a hurry when he did get outside. He just sort of felt the saddle as he went up, and when he did get in the middle of it he didn't start Big-Enough in a wild run and go whooping it up. Instead his head was down and his eyes and fingers kept going over all the good leather that was under, back and in front of him. It seemed as he rode away that he had a hunch that in such a rig as he was now sitting was where he'd be spending the biggest part of the many years ahead of him.

Billy was still letting Big-Enough poke along towards the big pasture and looking at his new saddle when Lem and his wife came around the corner of the stable and stood there watching him.

"Did you ever see a kid like that, Mary?" said Lem. "If there ever was a thoroughbred that kid sure is one, a thoroughbred cowboy."

Billy was sitting on top of the world and the meadowlarks that sang around him as he rode were right in tune with the beats of his heart. Like a true cowboy, while a good horse and saddle were under him, he wouldn't have traded places with any prince or king. It wasn't until Billy closed the corral gate on the cows and unsaddled his horse that he got to thinking how come he got his new saddle. The sight of it had left him pretty dumb and he'd not thought much of who brought it to him. Billy wasn't much on showing affection so he more than surprised his Dad and Mother when he did his best to hug one and then the other.

"By golly, Dad," he said, "That's sure a fine saddle and I'll work hard to pay you for it."

Chapter Six

Billy and Big-Enough covered a lot of territory that fall and the rest of the year. Of course the territory wasn't so big and no ride was made that was any farther than the big pasture. Once in a while when Billy would see his dad bringing in a bunch of cattle, he would ride out to meet him and help him corral them.

The boy and the horse had got to be great partners. By the time winter came there was a good polish on Billy's saddle, and a couple of little white spots on Big-Enough's back to show that he'd packed that saddle many a mile, but there were no sores on the round back. Lem had showed Billy how to saddle his horse a couple of times. He handed him a coarse woven saddle blanket so the air would circulate and showed him how to put it on and smooth off all wrinkles and how to feed, water and take care of his horse, so he would always be fresh and in good shape.

Billy did all of that well and when Christmas came that year he was rewarded by a fine pair of bearskin chaps and a little pair of boots. With the warm chaps and boots he was able to be out more that winter than any before. Only blizzards kept him inside and the rest of the time he was often out with his dad, helping him to bring in cattle that needed feeding.

Billy was getting to be quite a rider and an all-around cowboy. Around the horn of the little saddle were rope marks showing where the little rider had tried his hand at roping something or other and had made good catches.

With Christmas came a little pair of boots.

When time came to brand the cattle that spring Billy did his best to try to help. He was always by the branding fire and a couple of times he tried to pass a branding iron to his dad, but the handles were hot and the whole thing still too heavy for him. There was only one thing Billy could do at the branding time and that was to keep the fire going in good shape so the irons would keep hot. He made up for what he couldn't do as yet by watching and getting ready for the time when he could.

There were a couple of weeks of dull time for Billy after the branding was over. His dad and the other riders were making too long rides to take him along and there was no work of any kind left for him to do.

Then one day a strange rider brought in a big bunch of horses and from the bunch he cut out eight fine big four year old geldings. Billy was on the job and peeking through the corral bars. He had a hunch that there'd be something doing during the next few weeks.

And there was something doing. The rider had been hired by Lem and had brought the eight broncs in to break them to saddle.

Tied up and thinking it over

Billy saw everything that followed and that was plenty.

First watching the rider rope one wild range horse after another.

Letting each roped horse run on in the corral until he's jerked to a stop by the rope around the snubbing post.

Then when the horse throws himself, tying him down.

Letting him run around the snubbing post

Letting him up again with one hind foot tied up part ways, hindering his actions, and watching him fight until he found there was no winning by it.

Then fanning him with a gunny sack until the horse got used to the feel of it everywhere it touched him.

And finally riding him, with a little more fanning of the gunny sack.

Later using the quirt of wide flat leather, to take the buck out of him. This quirt doesn't sting and cut like the narrow one. It only scares the horse so that he quits his foolishness.

The breaking of all the broncs was started that way. All eight of them were handled and ridden a little every day, and after the second or third

The quirt takes the buck out of him.

saddling some of the broncs didn't need to have hobbles, but it was near two weeks before they'd tamed down and learned to go and stop, and turn many ways. Billy and Big-Enough rode out with Ned when he rode the broncs out to give them their daily ride and education.

When two weeks were up Ned had the broncs snapped out so that work could be done with them. All they needed was riding among the herds, where they'd have something to do and learn. A few would buck again off and on, but that was to be expected. Then Ned slapped his saddle on his only gentle horse, shook hands with Billy and Lem and rode on to tackle another string of broncs.

Billy watched him ride away and he sort of felt alone. He'd have nobody to ride and work with now, nobody that could make things as interesting and show him a wild time as Ned did with the broncs. He drew a long breath as he watched him ride out of sight around the point of a hill, and turning to Lem he said,

"Gee, Dad, Ned is sure a bronc-fighting fool, ain't he?"

Lem looked down at Billy, grinned and said,

"Yep, he's a good man all right."

Late that evening Billy was by the snubbing post in the breaking pen, practicing taking turns around it like Ned.

All they needed was riding among the herds.

Lem pointed down to where Billy was playing, “Look at that little codger, now,” he said to Mary. “We’ll have our hands full educating him to be anything else but what he is. If you brought an arithmetic book before him, he’d buck and snort and quit the flats.”

Bucking even harder than before

Watching the rider rope one wild range horse after another.

–Art courtesy of the Yellowstone Art Museum

Chapter Seven

One day during the fall when Billy was going on six years old his dad told him to saddle up, that he was going to take him along where the round-up wagon was camped, fifteen miles or so away.

Billy didn't linger to ask questions or to have the words repeated. He grabbed his clothes, lit out the door as if the house was afire, and went full-speed ahead for the corrals. He had Big-Enough caught and was slipping the saddle on him by the time his dad opened the corral gate.

Ten circuses couldn't have made any kid happier than Billy was at just the thought of seeing the round-up outfit. He'd heard his dad tell of such outfits many a time and of the work that went on.

They rode all day and Billy got to see further than he'd ever had a chance to see in his life. Presently they came to the round-up camp on the creek against the willows.

They rode all day.

Billy and his dad picketed their horses to graze close by and went into the camp. Billy followed Lem through the tarpaulin covered rolls of bedding up to where the cowmen were gathered, busy discussing things.

Being among all those men made Billy a little shy at first. Some saw that he didn't like to be asked such questions as "How old are you, Sonny?" or "Have you learned your A.B.C.'s yet?" So they began asking him more grown up questions like, "How did the stock winter in your country?" or "What make of saddle are you riding, Boy?" It made him feel right proud to answer these questions, especially when they asked him about his saddle. One asked him how many horses he had in his string, and Billy was kind of stumped for a spell. He didn't want to say that he had only one horse, so finally he said, "I got Big-Enough string"—and he meant that when he looked towards his horse grazing the length of the picket rope.

Finally the men left Billy to himself, and after he had listened to their talk for a spell he started to roam around the camp. He watched the cowboys come in, unsaddle, rope their night horses and picket them here and there on good grass. Billy watched the whole performance, and with watching other things around, it looked sometimes as if he'd about twist his head off.

There were around forty riders in camp when the cook hollered "Come and get it, you hyenas, or I'll throw it out." Tin plates, cups, knives and forks, salt and pepper and sugar were on the drop board of the chuck box; good hunks of range beef were in Dutch ovens; and in the other ovens were browned potatoes, hot biscuits, and gravy in the skillet.

There was no rush. Every rider waited for the other to take the lead, help himself, and take his time about it. All were hungry, but there was no pushing and shoving.

Billy had sidled up to his dad and watched how one rider after another helped himself to plate and cup and grub. When his time came he did it like

The chuck wagon

a man, so much like a man that nobody thought of helping him. His plate and cup filled, he picked a place where he could be by himself and watch the whole crowd. There on the sod he squatted like any good cowboy and began to get away with all he'd piled on the plate that rested between his knees, and, while his dad wasn't looking, he'd take sips of the black coffee that was in the cup and which he kept hid in the tall grass.

Along about sundown one of the cowboys dug out his mouth organ and, while all were gathered around the fire, he began playing songs that were sung all over the cow country at the time when the buffalo roamed over it. Many old timers picked up the tunes and went to humming, and then one cowboy and another started singing.

Finally the fire burned low, the mouth organ was put away, the singing stopped, and riders began to scatter out to their beds, unroll them and crawl in. Lem, seeing Billy so wide awake and interested in everything, thought he'd let the boy have a night of it. Instead of telling him to come to bed he just pointed out where the bed would be, telling him to come when he was ready. It was almost midnight before he came to where his dad was, and crawled in.

Chapter Eight

It seemed to Billy that he'd no more than just turned in when the cook's loud holler was heard. He didn't budge for awhile. Pretty soon he heard the crackling of the fire and then voices coming from here and there. The camp was coming to life.

It didn't take long for Billy to dress. All he'd taken off when he crawled into bed was his hat and coat and his overalls and boots. He was up, washed and alongside his dad before the cook told the crowd to "go to it, cowboys," and it didn't take him long to get his breakfast down.

Every rider in camp was at the herd when Billy and Big-Enough got there. It was the biggest herd that'd been put in one bunch that year and numbered around four thousand head. It was pretty nearly too big a herd to work all at once, but with all the riders on hand it could be managed. So the work started. The cattle belonging to the big outfit were cut out first because they made up more than half the herd. Then each neighboring cowman and his riders took their turn cutting out their own cattle from the strays that were left. When one cowman was through, he took his cattle far enough to one side so there wouldn't be a chance of any getting away and mixing with the herd. Then leaving one rider with them, he'd ride back to the main herd and help the others.

Billy had quite a time keeping out of the way when he first rode up to the herd. If a critter came towards him he'd try to dodge and give it a clear run. Then he'd turn his horse the wrong way and the animal would go back in the herd. So Lem rode up to him and told him to keep his horse still and the critter wouldn't notice him.

"There's only one thing," said Lem. "Keep away from fighting bulls, because the one that gets whipped don't care much what he goes through when he makes his get-away, and your horse might be standing in his road."

There were lots of bulls fighting in that big herd. Billy watched the way each man and horse worked. Once in a while there'd be some argument among the cowmen as to a brand on a certain critter. The brand would be dim, or crooked, or blotched so it couldn't be read very well. One would say it was this and the other one would say it was that. There was only one way to try and settle such arguments, and that was to rope and throw the animal. Then the hair was ruffled and the brand and earmark was looked at close.

Billy liked to see the ropers do their work on the big cattle, for the big cattle sure could hit the end of a rope and make it sing, and a couple of times a horse was jerked down.

It was along about the middle of the forenoon, or a little after, when the whole herd was worked and the strays were claimed by their owners. An early meal was spread. All hands took to it, and then, after a lot of handshaking and "I'll see you next year" or "At shipping time," the cowmen and their riders started for home.

Lem had over two hundred head of cattle to take back to his home range. He had a man to help him take them through the timber. And it was a good thing he had that help because there were quite a few bunch quitters in the herd. These were bound to cause trouble when timber was reached, leaving the herd and having to be chased back to it again.

Billy didn't have much chance to show his skill at turning back bunch quitters. He was put to bringing up the drags at the back end of the herd. But

There were lots of bulls fighting in that big herd.

a good chance came his way anyway. The cattle were trailing along through the timber. Billy had been watching a big cow which had been trying time and again to make a get-away, only to be turned back by his dad or the rider. But that old heifer was wise and had nowhere near given up trying. She began lagging behind and watching all the riders, and when she thought no one was looking, she dropped out and hightailed it for all she was worth for the thickest of the timber.

Billy just got a glimpse of the tip of her tail as she went, and, letting out a happy holler, he and Big-Enough sailed right after her. But Billy got all he wanted when he went to follow that cow. She could go thru places where the brush was low and he had to go around. His face and hands were getting scratched and his clothes were getting torn. His happy holler was lost to the winds and now he was gritting his teeth. But he was bound to head off that cow and bring her back even if it took him all day. He heard the cow breaking thru the thick timber and keeping to open country, he followed her by the noise she made. Then he saw a clearing ahead and he rode for it, figuring on heading her off there and turning her back. The cow came to the clearing. She had a wild look in her eyes as she stopped for a few seconds and sized up Billy and his horse. Then she came on and Big-Enough had to do some squirming to keep her horns out of his flanks. The old heifer was mad. She'd been turned a few times too often, and that didn't agree with her wild disposition. So after making a few passes at the horse she hightailed it on across the clearing and towards another patch of thick timber.

Billy had been scared when the cow made for him and his horse, and her horns grazed his legs, but now he suddenly got mad, too, and he lit right out after her. As long as the cow kept running he felt pretty safe. All he'd have to watch for was when she stopped and turned.

When she found herself in a narrow brushy canyon, the cow couldn't go further. There she turned and faced Billy.

The boy was stuck now as to what to do. She might rush him any second and he'd be lucky if he could keep out of her way in that narrow canyon. He rode away from her a short distance, figuring on letting the cow stay there and cool off a bit, thinking she'd get over her mad spell, then she would come out and he could drive her back to the herd.

But the cow had no such intentions. She had a bad heart and when Billy turned his horse she came on, with no idea of being stopped.

It was just as the cow was boosting Billy and Big-Enough out of the canyon when there was a crashing of dry limbs and up came Lem on his big gray horse. One glance at the goings-on and, seeing the danger Billy was in, Lem saw red. He uncoiled his rope and like a streak of lighting he was up on the cow. She made a pass at his horse as he let her by and then a loop settled on her horns. Lem had kept his horse on a tight run. The cow was on the run too as she passed him, and both were going opposite directions. In the wink of an eye both had come to the end of the rope and the cow sure got the worst of it. Her head was brought to snap alongside of her tail; she was raised four feet off the ground, and when she landed she popped like the lash of a bull whip.

She didn't get up for a while. Lem gave her slack and let her come to. His eyes were afire as he waited, and he didn't dare look at Billy. When the cow got up she'd lost all of her fighting spirit, and seemed to have put all of her heart into being docile.

"I'll make a pet of you," said Lem as he popped her on the nose with the end of his rope and turned her towards the herd. Lem was still mad as a hornet

She made a pass at his horse and then a loop settled on her horns.

Her head was brought to snap alongside of her tail,
she was raised four feet off the ground.

and it was hard for him to smile as Billy rode alongside of him. The sight of that cow rushing at his boy had scared him so that when he did get at her he just went on a wild rampage. He didn't cool down much until he got near the herd and saw the cow edge her way into the middle of it. She'd never quit the herd again and never turn on a rider.

When the herd was started on the way again he looked at Billy and grinned.

"You could have got that cow in by yourself, Billy. She was sure learning to follow you."

Billy didn't know whether to grin at that or not. He'd been the one who was doing the getting away when his dad rode up. Well, anyway, his dad hadn't caught him riding back and letting the cow go. Such doings don't set well on a rider's reputation as a cowboy.

Lem rode to the side of the herd and Billy had new eyes for him as he watched him. He'd never seen his dad do any but ordinary and quiet roping while around the corrals at home. The way he'd handled that big mad cow and tossed her around like a bag of peanuts had been a surprise to Billy. That was about as pretty and reckless a piece of roping as could be seen.

"I'll bet," said Billy to himself, "that he can ride a bronc as good as Ned, too."

When they were through the timber, the herd was left to scatter among the rolling hills that led up to tall mountains where there was plenty of water and strong feed.

The three riders stopped their horses, watched the cattle for a spell, then rode on for the ranch. It was dark when they got there but cheerful lights were burning at the ranch house and at the cook house, when they rode in.

There was one tired and hungry, but smiling and happy little cowboy that night under Lem Roper's roof.

Chapter Nine

As winter came and all the weaker and older cattle were brought close to the ranch where they could be watched, there got to be less and less riding. It was during a spell of nothing much to do that Billy was introduced to the A.B.C.'s.

Billy didn't shy at the book at first. It was stormy outside and he couldn't see the hills anyway. So he listened to his mother explaining what the funny marks on paper were and why he should learn to read them. She got his interest by telling him that a good many of the marks were used for the brands and that he'd have to learn the names of them so he could tell what the brand was. Billy would rather have learned the marks by reading from the hide of a cow than from a book, but his mother said it would take a long time before he would see as many brands as there were in the book, and he'd better learn them now so he would know.

In winter. —Art courtesy
of the Yellowstone Art Museum

With the coaching of his mother Billy soon got to find that by putting a few brands together a word would be made. One day he stumped his mother by asking where his dad's brands were in the book. Lem's cattle brand was one called Rafter-hook and his horse brand was Square-Dot . Billy's mother had quite a time figuring that out but she finally did it by taking letters and spelling out the words–

R-A-F-T-E-R H-O-O-K
S-Q-U-A-R-E D-O-T

This seemed to satisfy Billy, though he couldn't figure out why it should take so many letters to spell a brand when the brand itself could be made so easily.

After a time Billy knew all the brands from A to Z. He didn't see the need of bunching them and trying to make words–and about this time his studying was getting to be work. Then he stumbled on something that made him take a new interest. One day when he was in the bunkhouse he found a book with the picture of a saddle on the cover. He opened the book and inside were pictures of more saddles and then chaps, boots, fancy spurs and bits, hats, ropes, and everything to attract the cowboy's eye.

Pictures of everything to attract the cowboy's eye

It was a saddlery catalog, the first Billy had ever seen, and for a long hour he kept his nose between the pages of it. There were sure some pretty saddles to look at and everything else was pretty. He wished he had a pair of spurs like this or that and wished for many other things in the book. Then he got to wondering what the words beneath each article said. He wished he knew, but his mother would know, so he borrowed the catalog and hit on home with it.

His mother wasn't slow in helping the sudden interest that Billy took in the new book. He never seemed to get tired of it, and for fear he might some time, Mary got to hiding it and told him he could only have it at certain times when she could look it over with him.

Before spring came, Billy knew how to spell and pronounce many of the words in the catalog, bigger words than in the A.B.C. book.

Lem sat down at the table one night and wrote all the saddle makers he'd heard of asking for their catalogs. A couple of weeks later, Jim, happening to ride by from the post-office, dropped about twenty pounds of saddle catalogs on Lem's house porch.

"Gee-whillikins," said Jim as he dropped the heavy parcel, "you sure must be going to spread yourself to some new riggings, Lem."

"Not by a long shot," said Lem, grinning. "These are Billy's new school books."

The catalogs were all sizes. They were well illustrated with photographs and drawings and no two were alike. Billy took to them as Big-Enough would take to his oats, and Mary found herself a mighty busy reader.

By middle summer Billy could read and spell and know the meanings of such words as

ROSADERO GUARANTEE
SPECIFICATIONS TAPADERO

And so on. He knew the name of the states where the catalogs came from, and he could add the price of all the things he'd seen that he'd like to have.

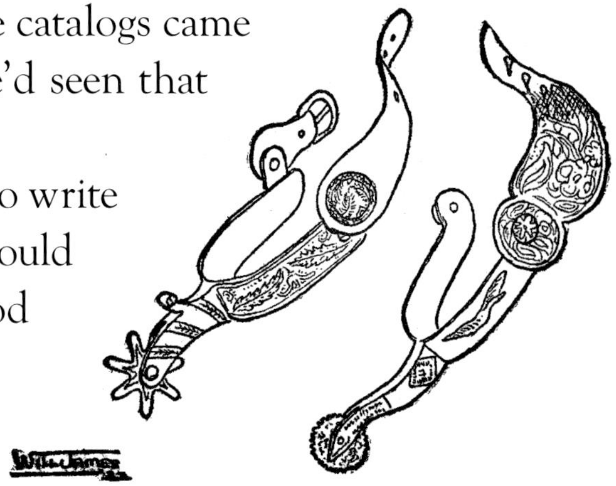

One day Lem told him that if he would learn to write an order by hand and do it so it could be read, he would let him order any pair of spurs he saw. Billy had good taste and he picked a twenty-five dollar pair, the kind that would fit him, too. Lem couldn't back out on the agreement so Billy went to work getting his mother to teach him how to write.

It took some months before he could write the order so it was readable. The scribble didn't follow the lines very well and took about all the order blank. Later when Billy wasn't looking Lem wrote the order for the spurs over again.

As time passed Billy went on taking more time to his catalog education. One good reason was he wanted a silver mounted bit to match his spurs, and his dad told him he'd have to write a heap better order than the last one before he could get the bit. By early spring he finally made out an order that surprised and pleased Lem, and this one didn't have to be made over.

The bit came in good time. Lem kept it hidden for a few days and then handed it to Billy on his birthday. It was a fine bit and Billy had hardly unwrapped it when he rushed down to the stable and tried it on Big-Enough to see how it would look. It was Big-Enough's birthday too, or mighty close to it one way or the other, and after the bit was tried and put away, Billy scooped him a feed of grain.

Chapter Ten

With all the studying Billy did he still found time to be in the saddle and on Big-Enough nearly as much as before. The only difference now was that he did very little aimless riding, and when he saddled up it was to go on some good long and interesting ride with his dad or the other riders. He could handle the irons better when branding time came, too. If he disappeared for a spell Lem and Mary didn't worry about him as they used to. Billy was only going on seven but he was able to think clearer and take care of himself better than most kids at ten.

Big-Enough, for a horse, was far ahead of Billy in learning. He was now a full grown horse weighing nine-hundred pounds.

As fall came on Lem took Billy to the round-up wagon again for two days this time. He was fast improving as a cowboy and Big-Enough sure wasn't letting up any as a cowhorse. Billy's dad had given him another horse now, larger than Big-Enough.

One day Billy was riding his big horse on a high lope towards home when the horse struck one front foot in a hole and turned over a few times. In the scramble Billy broke his wrist. When the horse got up one of Billy's silver mounted spurs caught in the rope and there he hung by his heel. The horse got scared then, and started to run and kick. Billy bounced up and down and dragged, getting bruised and scratched. He thought sure the end had come. He thought of many things all at once. But somehow he didn't get scared and he didn't let one holler out of him. Then something bumped him and all went dark.

He thought sure the end had come.

When he woke up he tried to raise himself to look around and see where he was, and remembered things. He used the wrong arm to raise himself on and then a sharp pain made him remember how his wrist snapped while his horse fell. He used the other arm and, sitting up a bit, saw that one of his boots was gone. He was stiff and sore, but he finally managed to stand up and start limping toward home. It wasn't over a mile or so away and that was good. A little way on he found his other boot. He was glad to see the spur was still on it, and even though it hurt some he slipped the boot on. He walked better after that.

Nobody had seen the horse packing the empty saddle come in at the ranch. So when Billy finally walked into the house all bloody and ragged, he stirred quite a commotion. His mother, who had seen and helped many a hurt rider, nearly fainted at the first glance of him.

But it wasn't long before she stood up and began doing something. When Lem came in a while later Billy had been all washed up and had splints bandaged around his wrist. Lem got a good deal lighter under his tan when Mary started telling him what had happened and he rushed out of the house and hollered to one of the cowboys, "Corral and hook up that fast team as soon as possible."

Town was forty-five miles away over hills and rolling country. "We'll be there in two or three hours," said Lem, trying to cheer Mary up. "And don't worry now. Billy is all right and we'll rush him in just so the doctor can set his wrist before it swells too much."

The team was hooked up in fast time. Lem, Mary and Billy hopped in the buckboard. Lem took the lines and away they went. The team was kept in a fast trot most of the way and sometimes into a long lope. That pleased Billy, and once in a while when the team was held down to a walk and going up a steep hill Lem would pass remarks that pleased him some more.

"You'll soon be fit as a fiddle again, little cowboy," he said. "The only thing you'll just have to be careful and have to stay in town for a spell. You won't mind that, will you? There'll be

Town was reached in less than three hours.

lots of funny things for you to see in town and I'll sure take good care of Big-Enough while you're away. If you'd been riding him you wouldn't of got hurt, but you can't be riding him all the time, can you?"

Billy would answer his dad's questions with crooked grins. It was kind of hard to grin.

Town was reached in less than three hours. Billy's wrist was set and put in a cast, and late that night he was with his mother and dad in the room of the main hotel, feeling a little sick, and not at all wanting his share of a well-spread meal that was ordered.

The next morning Lem had a long talk with Mary. Then with "I'll be riding in every couple of weeks or so," he shook Billy's good hand and started back for the ranch. He'd be eating at the cook house with his cowboys for some months because Mary would be staying in town for the whole winter. Lem and Mary had decided that it would be a good time to start Billy to school.

Chapter Eleven

Billy took to school in as scary a way as a raw snorty bronc takes to a corral. With his arm still in a sling he started studying the strange herd of other youngsters around him. The first days weren't so dull. His arm being in a sling and his telling the kids how he came to hurt it, set him up as quite a hero among them. The other kids, even though they lived in a town in the heart of good cow country, knew very little about ranch life. Very few of them had ever been on a horse or knew much about them. Their interest was more in the new bicycle that big brother had. Their fun was playing with a ball, buying candy, and going to shows. Billy tried his best to get some fun out of their way of playing. He did have some fun sometimes, but always there was that hankering for the hills and the feel of his saddle and horse under him.

One day his mother let him buy a rope, and that helped some. He took it to school and played with it while the other kids played games. He had his own way of playing, just as they did. The rope and the way Billy could handle it, even with his left arm in a sling, drew a lot of attention from some of the kids. Soon there began to appear more ropes, all kinds, and many a back yard got to be without a clothes line.

After the first few days of school Billy began to get used to things. He was liked by the teacher and most of the boys and girls, and there were a few boys he began to run with pretty steady. He wasn't strong with the girls. He felt sort of uncomfortable when one come near, and even tho many a smile from pig-tailed heads came his way, he couldn't mix in their company as easily as the other boys did.

As far as his start on education was concerned he had the other kids stumped and the teacher surprised. The other kids were writing such words as cat and rabbit when he could take tongue-twisters like chinkadero and qualification.

With his saddle catalogs and the help of his school books Billy got to learning quite a bit more that winter. He could write a letter and order in pretty fine shape by the time spring came. He thought of how his first saddle had seen plenty of use, how it was getting thin in places and it would soon be time for

He wondered how Big-Enough had wintered and what he looked like.

a new one, so he put in a lot of work writing and rewriting letters, and trying to describe the kind of new saddle he wanted. When the trees began to leaf out around town, Billy figured that the last order and letter he wrote would do. He stuck that in an envelope, addressed it, and tucked it away to show his dad when he got back home.

Billy was anxious to see his dad again in his chaps instead of town clothes, at home, by the corrals and in the hills where there were cattle and horses to see instead of buildings and smoky skylines. He wondered how Big-Enough had wintered and what he looked like.

Big-Enough had come in from the pasture that evening.

It seemed a long spell between Spring break up and the month of June. Finally with hours going by as slow as whole days the time did come for the school house door to close for the summer. Billy was the first out that door, and after saying goodbye to a few boys, and smiling to a couple of girls, he hit a high lope for the house where he and his mother had been staying.

It was a great surprise, and Billy dropped his books and hollered, when, as he came in the house, he saw his dad standing by his mother. He'd come in the buckboard this time, to take them home.

The ride to the ranch was different than the one they'd taken the fall before. Billy's broken wrist had mended well, and there was no crooked smile on his face now as he looked at the country around. When the buckboard pulled in at the ranch the place looked sort of strange. It was the same place, sure enough and he knew every pole and log in the corrals, stables and houses, but the whole outfit looked so much better and prettier, and even the air seemed to smell sweeter.

Billy was like a fellow who's just come out after many months in a hospital or jail. He had new eyes for the ranch, and till way after dark that evening he kept smelling the air, listening to the rustle of leaves, the fall of the stream, and all the good things that made a sound. His eyes had roamed all over the place, his fingers had touched corral timbers and saddle leather and, to top off that day perfect, Big-Enough had come in from the pasture that evening—Billy was home again.

Chapter Twelve

Billy was a born cowboy; the only kind that ever makes the real cowboy. One day Lem told him he could have a certain black horse if he could break him. It was a little black horse, pretty as a picture. Billy went wild at the sight of him, and ran into the corral to get as close a view of the horse as he could.

"By golly!" he said. "I've always wanted to break in a horse. That'll be lots of fun."

The next morning Lem found Billy in the corral with the new horse.

"Well, I see you're busy right early, Billy."

"You bet, you," he said. "He's some horse, ain't he?"

"He sure is," agreed Lem. "And your first bronc, too."

An hour or so later Billy had his saddle on the black horse, and cinched to stay. By this time quite a crowd had gathered around. The foreman, the cowboys, all the ranch hands were watching. All was set but taking the hobbles off the horse's front feet and climbing on. Some of the men offered to do that for Billy but that young cowboy refused. He wanted to do it all himself; it was his bronc.

Billy gathered his hackamore rope and a hunk of mane to go with it, grabbed the saddle horn with his right hand and, sticking his foot in the stirrup, eased himself into the saddle. He squirmed around until he was well set, like an old bronc fighter saw that the length of the reins between his hands and the pony's head was just right, then he reached over and pulled off the blindfold.

Billy's lips were closed tight; he was ready for whatever happened. The pony blinked at seeing daylight again, looked back at the boy sitting on him, snorted, and trotted off.

A laugh went up from all around. Billy turned a blank face toward his father and hollered,

"Hey, Dad, he won't buck!"

WILL JAMES '30

Another laugh was heard and when it quieted down Lem spoke up.

"Never mind, son," he said trying to keep a straight face, "he might buck yet."

The words were no more than out of his mouth, when the little black lit into bucking. Billy was loosened the first jump for he'd been paying more attention to what his dad was saying than to what he was sitting on. The little pony crowhopped around the corral and bucked just enough to keep the kid from getting back in the saddle. Billy was hanging on to all he could find, but pretty soon the little old pony happened to make the right kind of a jump for the kid and he straightened up again.

Billy rode pretty fair the next few jumps and managed to keep his seat pretty well under him, but he wasn't satisfied with just sitting there; he grabbed his hat and began fanning. All went fine for a few more jumps and then trouble broke loose. Billy dropped his hat and made a wild grab for the saddle horn.

But the hold on the saddle horn didn't help him any; he kept going, up and up he went, a little higher every jump, and pretty soon he started coming down. When he did that he was by his lonesome. The horse had gone in another direction.

"Where is he?" said Billy, trying to get some of the earth out of his eyes.

"Right here, Son," said his father, who'd caught the horse and brought him up.

He handed the kid the hackamore reins and touched him on the hand.

"And listen here, young feller, if I catch you grabbing the horn with that paw of yours again, I'll tie it and the other right back where you can't use 'em."

Those few words hit the kid pretty hard. There was a frown on his face and his lips were quivering at the same time. He was both ashamed and peeved.

His father held the horse while Billy climbed on again.

"Are you ready, cowboy?" Lem looked up at his son and smiled.

After some efforts the kid smiled back and answered,

"Yes, Dad, let him go."

The pony lit into bucking the minute he was loose this time and seemed to mean business from the start. Time and again Billy's hand reached down as if to grab the saddle horn, but he kept away from it.

The little horse was bucking pretty good, and for a kid Billy was doing mighty fine, but the horse still proved too much for him. Billy kept getting further and further away from the saddle till finally he slid along the pony's shoulder and to the ground once again.

The kid was up before his dad could get to him and he began looking for his horse right away.

"I don't think you'd better try to ride him any more today, Sonny," Lem said as he brushed some of the dust off the kid's clothes. "Maybe tomorrow you can ride him easy."

But Billy turned and saw the horse challenging him, it seemed, and he crossed the corral, caught the black, blindfolded him and climbed him again.

Then Lem walked up to Billy and said so nobody else could hear,

"You go after him this time, Billy, and just make this pony think you're the wolf of the world. Paw him the same as you did that last calf you rode."

The little horse was bucking pretty good.

"Y-e-e-ep!" Billy hollered as he jerked the blind off the pony's eyes. "I'm a wolf!"

Billy was a wolf; he'd turned challenger and was pawing the black from ears to rump. Daylight showed plenty between him and the saddle but somehow he managed to stick on and stay right side up. The horse, surprised at the change of events, finally let up on his bucking; he was getting scared and had found a sudden hankering to start running.

After that it was easy for Billy; he rode him around the corral a couple of times and then, all smiles and proud as a peacock, he climbed off.

Billy had ridden his first bronc.

Will James was born Joseph Ernest Nephtali Dufault in Quebec on June 6, 1892. He left home as a teenager to live out his dream of becoming a cowboy in the American West. James went on to write and illustrate twenty-four books and numerous magazine articles about horses, cowboying, and the West. He died in 1942, at the age of fifty.